P9-DGE-322

Apples and Pumpkins

by Anne Rockwell

pictures by Lizzy Rockwell

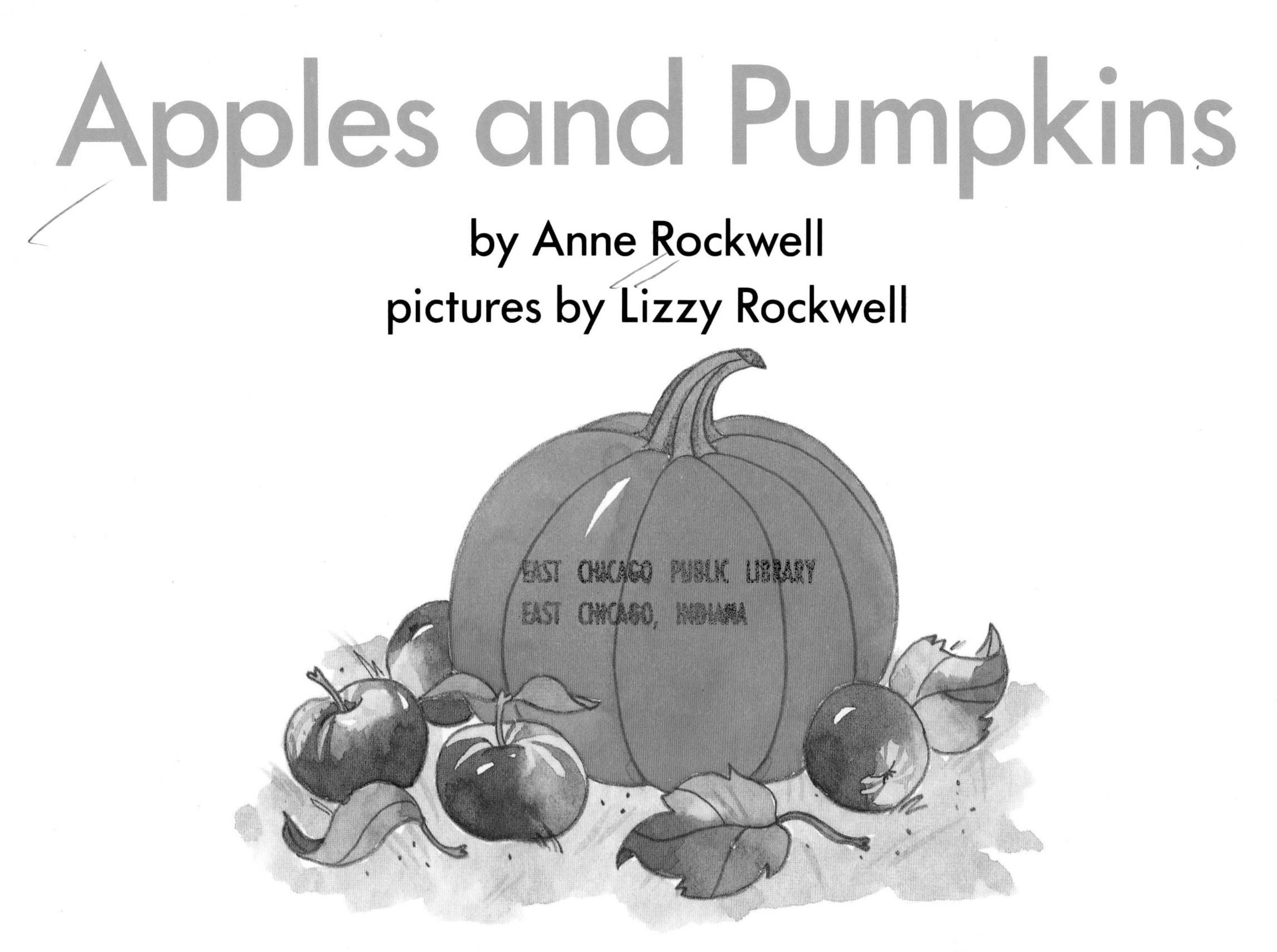

MACMILLAN PUBLISHING COMPANY · NEW YORK

COLLIER MACMILLAN PUBLISHERS · LONDON

For Lucrezia and Ludovica

Macmillan Publishing Company
866 Third Avenue, New York, NY 10022
Collier Macmillan Canada, Inc.
Printed and bound in Singapore
First American Edition

10 9 8 7 6 5 4

The text of this book is set in 24 point Spartan Book.
The illustrations are rendered in pencil and watercolor.

Library of Congress Cataloging-in-Publication Data

Rockwell, Anne F. Apples and pumpkins
by Anne Rockwell; pictures by Lizzy Rockwell.—1st American ed. p. cm.
Summary: In preparation for Halloween night, a family visits
Mr. Comstock's farm to pick apples and pumpkins.
ISBN 0-02-777270-5
[1. Halloween—Fiction. 2. Apple—Fiction. 3. Pumpkin—Fiction.]
I. Rockwell, Lizzy, ill. II. Title.
PZ7.R5943Ap 1989 [E]—dc19 88-22628 CIP AC

When red and yellow leaves
are on the trees,

we go to the Comstock Farm

to pick apples and pumpkins.

Mr. Comstock gives us
a bushel basket
to put our apples in.

Geese and chickens
and a big, fat turkey
walk with us
on our way to the orchard
where the apples grow.

My father picks apples.
My mother does, too.

I climb into a little apple tree
and pick the reddest apples of all.

When our basket is full
of red and shiny apples,

we go to the field
where the pumpkins grow.

I look and look
until I find
the best pumpkin of them all.

My father cuts it
from the vine.

I carry it
back to the car.

At home we carve
a jack-o'-lantern face
on our big, orange pumpkin.

We put a candle inside and light it.
Now our pumpkin looks scary
and funny, too.

On Halloween night
we put our pumpkin on the doorstep.
My mother gives away lots of
our red and shiny apples
for trick or treat,

while I go trick-or-treating
up and down our street.